Anonymous

The Star Games, Tricks and Puzzles

Anonymous

The Star Games, Tricks and Puzzles

ISBN/EAN: 9783337038137

Printed in Europe, USA, Canada, Australia, Japan

Cover: Foto ©Andreas Hilbeck / pixelio.de

More available books at **www.hansebooks.com**

THE STAR

.MES, TRICKS AND PUZZLES.

r Publishing Company,

JERSEY CITY, N. J.

PRICE, 25 CENTS.

) BY W. T. KIGHTLINGER. 1893.

GAMES

THE GAME OF CLUMPS.

Divide your company into two parts, in different rooms within sound of each other. Each room chooses one of their number. The two chosen go by themselves and agree upon some article with which all are familiar, which the others must guess. It may be the church bell, the clock, a certain tree or flower, or picture, or house, or river. It may be something quite insignificant, a pin in a certain place, a nail in one's shoe. The smaller the article the harder it is to guess.

Whatever is chosen it must be something definite; for instance, you must not choose a pin simply, but the pin in Bessie's hat, or the nail in the barn door.

If the two parties are seated in the parlors, say, the girl chosen by the front parlor goes into the back room, and the back parlor girl goes into the front room. As soon as they appear, each company begins to ask questions about the article they are to guess; for instance, they ask is it animal, mineral or vegetable? Is it square, round or flat? Is it hard or soft, liquid or solid? Is it black, white or blue? etc. Is it in this town, on this street, in this room? Any question may be asked that can be correctly answered by yes or no. As soon as one party guesses the word they all clap their hands to let the other party know it. Of course they are the victorious party.

GAME CALLED FREE MASONS.

The leader selects a person to be blindfolded. While the handkerchief is being tied on some one appointed by the leader slyly pins a handkerchief on the back of the one blinded, the leader meantime asking, " Do you wish to join the Free Masons ? " " Yes, I do." The leader then says, " There is a handkerchief put in a certain place in this room ; if you can find it you may join."

The blindfold is now taken off, and much amusement is caused by his efforts to find the handkerchief.

MUSICAL CHAIR.

Have one chair less than the players. Place them back and front alternately. The players march around them to the sound of some sort of music, which, suddenly stopping, they try to get a chair. The one failing must pay a pawn.

" POOR PUSSY."

A game which will make everyone laugh is " Poor Pussy." The company sit on one side of the room. One is chosen to be "Pussy," and stands before the first one and meows like a cat. The one sitting must look into " Pussy's " face, and without laughing, say, "Poor Pussy !" If they do not laugh, " Pussy " must pass on to the next one and so on. The laugher must become " Pussy." Continue this way until all have been meowed at.

THE COTTON FLIES.

One takes a bit of cotton or down, and casts it into the air. He puffs to keep it in the air. The one towards whom it floats must puff to keep it from falling into his lap, which would cost him a forfeit.

It is very amusing to see ten or twelve upturned faces, puffing each his own way to send the cotton from one to the other. As one cannot well laugh and puff at the same time, the cotton may fall into his mouth. Then for a general laughter and a demand of him for a forfeit for his gluttony.

2

HUNT THE RING.

A long tape with a ring on it is held by one of the players (who stands in a circle with one in the middle). The ring is passed swiftly from hand to hand. The middle one must find it and seize the hand holding it. The players make his task hard by pretending to pass it along when it is really in another part of the circle. The owner of the hand found to have it must now be the middle man.

GUESSING.

One goes out. Some object in the room is chosen by all. The questioner calls the one who is out and begins, "Is it the carpet or anything else?" The answer will be "No" until the questioner names something with four legs, the one following that is the one chosen. The answerer being instructed by the questioner beforehand always knows when to say "Yes." This is a great surprise to those who do not know the secret.

FRUIT BASKET.

Sit in a circle. One stands in the centre. Each takes the name of a fruit—orange, grape, etc. The centre calls the name of the fruit; if he does it three times before the owner of the name says it once, she must give him her seat. If he says "Fruit Basket," all must change seats, and the centre may get one if he can. The loser must now be the centre.

CATCH QUESTIONS.

It is always a delight to a school-boy to propound to his teacher "catch questions" in mathematics that the teacher cannot answer. Usually these "catch questions" or propositions, are of little importance, and the object of them is simply to elicit absurd replies from those to whom they are put.

We give several such questions, a few of which are new, and the others as "old as the hills," but new, probably, to some school-boys and girls.

If a goose weighs ten pounds and a half its own weight, what is the weight of the goose? Who has not been tempted to reply on the instant, fifteen pounds?—the correct answer being, of course, twenty pounds. Indeed, it is astonishing what a very simple query will sometimes catch a wise man napping; even the following have been known to succeed:

How many days would it take to cut up a piece of cloth fifty yards long, one yard being cut off every day?

A snail climbing up a post twenty feet high, ascends five feet every day, and slips down four feet every night. How long will the snail take to reach the top of the post?

A wise man having a window one yard high and one yard wide, and requiring more light, enlarged his window to twice its former size, yet the window was still only one yard high and one yard wide. How was this done?

This is a catch question in geometry, as the preceding were catch questions in arithmetic. The window was diamond shaped at first, and was afterwards made square.

As to the former, perhaps it is not necessary to point out that the answer to the first is not fifty days, but forty-nine; and to the second, not twenty days, but sixteen—since the snail, who gains one foot for fifteen days, climbs on the sixteenth day to the top of the pole, and there remains.

CROSS-QUESTIONS AND CROOKED ANSWERS.

The company sit round, and each one whispers a question to his neighbor on the right, and then each one whispers an answer; so that each answers the question propounded by some other player, and of the purport of which he is entirely ignorant. Then every player has to recite the question he received from one player and the answer he got from the other, and the ridiculous incongruity of these random cross questions and crooked

4

answers will frequently excite a good deal of sport. One, for instance, may say, "I was ask if I considered dancing agreeable?" and the answer was, "Yesterday fortnight." Another may declare, "I was ask if I had seen the comet?" and the answer was, "He was married last year!" A third, "I was asked what I liked best for dinner?" and the answer was, "The Emperor of China!"

MY LADIES TOILET.

Each person represents some necessary article of the toilet—brush, comb, soap, scent, broach, jewel-case, etc., and the lady's maid stands in the middle of the circle and calls for any article her lady is supposed to want. The personator of that article must then jump up, or be fined a forfeit for negligence. Every now and then the abigail announces that her lady wants her whole toilet, when the whole circle of players must rise and change places. The lady's maid herself makes a bolt for a chair, and the player who is left chairless in the scuffle becomes lady's maid.

HUNT THE HARE.

The company all form a circle, holding each other's hands. One, called the hare, is left out, who runs several times around the ring, and at last stops, tapping one of the players on the shoulder. The one tapped quits the ring and runs after the hare, the circle again joining hands. The hare runs in and out in every direction, passing under the arms of those in the circle, until caught by the pursuer, when he becomes hare himself. Those in the circle must always be friends to the hare, and assist its escape in every way possible.

5

GAME OF PROVERBS.

One leaves the room so they cannot hear what is said. A proverb is chosen. He returns and begins with the first one in the ring, asking a question. The answer must include the first word of the proverb. The next answers with the second word of the proverb, and so on.

If now the questioner guesses the proverb, he must name the one who made him think of it. That one must takes his place.

RETURNING BORROWED PROPERTY.

The more players the better. They sit in a ring. Two are selected, one of whom goes round, giving each a name; that is, Tom is "Needle-work," Jane, "A False Tooth." The second follows, telling each to take another to a third. Tom must carry Lottie to Grandpa, saying, "I bring back what I borrowed." Grandpa inquires, "What did you borrow?" Tom must give his own name, "A needlework."

Ingenuity in naming players, and in selecting opposites to take one another around make this very amusing.

Once a gentleman carried the prettiest girl to another gentleman, saying he had returned, "A Toad with a fly in its mouth," which brought forth peals of laughter.

AN OLD SOLDIER COMING TO TOWN.

The words "black" or "white," "yes" or "no," must not be used in answering.

The leader says to one, "An old soldier is coming to town. What will you give him?" The answer may be "Peanuts." The leader questions about them, and asks if she cannot give something else; she says "yes," and gives the name of something else. The leader must try to make her say one of the four words. Failing, he must go to the next one. The answerer using one of these words, must now question.

OVERTURNED WITH A BREATH.

Lay on the edge of the table a long and narrow paper bag, and place some heavy weights, two dictionaries, for example, upon the closed end. The books can be overturned without being touched, simply by blowing.

The compressed air will swell the bag so violently that the weights upon it will be raised and thrown over. This experiment enables us to measure the strength of our breath by overturning objects of various weights and will prove that an adult can, without fatigue, raise with his breath, a weight of at least twenty pounds.

GAME OF QUESTIONS.

Played in a circle, each with paper and pencil. One asks at least ten questions. Players write answers. The one who asked the questions collects and reads them aloud. Players try to guess the name of writers.

THE FEATHER GAME.

Let the players sit in a circle, with chairs close together. The leader blows a feather upward toward the centre. The company must keep it afloat with their breaths. Its falling involves forfeits to the one on whom or near whom it falls.

BASE.

Two choose sides. Each side now gathers at its "base" or post, twenty yards apart, with a "dare" mark three yards from the base. Then one goes to the dare mark of the other side, when they rush to catch him. If caught he plays on the other side. The party gaining all is victorious.

MEMORY GAMES.

The players sit in a circle. One who knows the game begins with number one, "One old ox." This is repeated by each in turn till it gets back to the leader, who says, "One old ox and two tantalizing tame toads." The leader adding a number and each beginning with the first and repeating all. The " Forgettor" must pay a penalty.

GAME OF BEASTS, BIRDS AND FISH.

One throws a small ball at another and says either beasts, birds or fishes. The receiver must mention a beast, bird or fish of the sort mentioned by the former before another can pick it up, and so on.

LETTER-BOX.

The company must sit in a circle. One, with paper and pencil, must write the names of cities she can think of (two or more names than players). Then she puts a cross by the one of the names she prefers, then passes the list to the next, who imitates her, and so on.

Then the first one, standing in the centre, calls out two or more of the names of the list, as "My letter goes between Boston and Lowell." Then the choosers of said names must change places, when the first one must try to take one of the vacant seats. The loser of the seat must now take the place of the first one and call out.

TRICKS

THE KENTUCKY GIANT.

Two persons represent the giant, and the method of enacting the part is best explained by the accompanying engraving. It will be seen that one boy puts on a *long* cloak, and perches himself on the shoulders of his companion, who arranges the folds of the cloak so that the parts shown by the

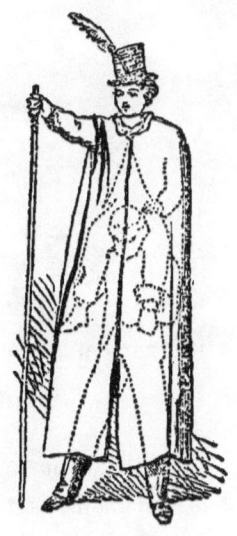

dotted lines in the illustration are entirely concealed from the eyes of the spectator. The boy who does the head and shoulders of the giant should carry a long staff as a cane, and if he wear a stove-pipe hat with a feather in it, it will greatly heighten the effect.

THE ELEPHANT.

Two boys are required to personate the elephant. The two boys place themselves as shown in the illustration : a quilt doubled over three or four times is now placed on the backs of the boys, which serves to form the back of the elephant; a large blanket or traveling shawl is then thrown over them, one end of which is twisted to represent the trunk of the animal, and the other end serving in a similar manner to represent the tail. Two

paper cones enact the tusks, and the elephant is complete. A bright and witty boy should be selected to perform the part of keeper, and he must lecture upon the prodigious strength, wonderful sagacity and extreme docility of the animal, proving the latter quality by lying down and permitting the elephant to walk over him. It always amuses a company to *show them the elephant.*

HOW TO STRIKE THE KNUCKLES WITHOUT HURTING THEM.

Select a marble mantel or any other hard surface; then tell the spectators that by a certain preparation you use you have made your knuckles so hard nothing can hurt them, in proof of which you offer to strike them on the marble slab of the mantel. To do this, you raise your fist firmly

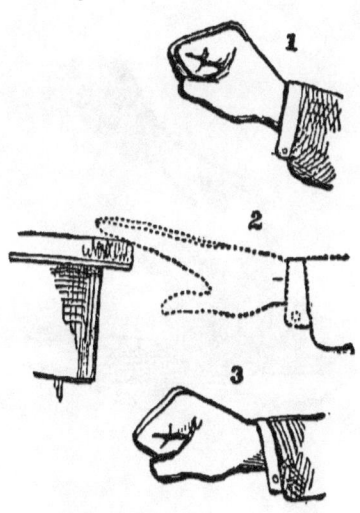

clenched above the mantel, and as you bring it rapidly down, open your fingers suddenly and strike the mantel, then close them again as represented in the engravings, 1, 2 and 3. If this is quickly done, you will seem to have knocked your knuckles violently.

HAT MEASUREMENT.

Very few people are aware of the height of the crown of a stove-pipe hat. A good deal of fun may be created by testing it in this way : Ask a person to point out on a wall about what he supposes to be the height of an ordinary hat, and he will place his finger usually at a height of about a foot from the ground. You then place a hat under it, and to his surprise

he finds that the space indicated is more than double the height of the hat. The height of a common flour barrel is just the length of a horse's face, and much fun may be derived from getting a company to mark the supposed height of a flour barrel. In nine cases out of ten they will mark many inches too high.

THE IMMOVABLE CARD.

Take an ordinary visiting card and bend down the ends as represented in the annexed figure; then ask any person to blow it over. This seems easy enough, but it may be tried for hours without succeeding. It is, however, to be done by blowing sharply on the table at some distance from the card.

TO BRING TWO SEPARATE COINS INTO ONE HAND.

Take two cents, which must be carefully placed in each hand, as thus: The right hand with the coin on the fourth and little finger, as in the illustration. Then place at a short distance from each other, both hands open on the table, the left palm being level with the fingers of the right. By now

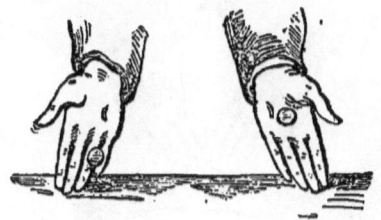

suddenly turning the hands over, the cent from the right hand will fly, without being perceived, into the palm of the left, and make the transit appear most unaccountable to the bewildered eyes of the spectators. By placing the audience in front and not at the side of the exhibitor, this illusion, if neatly performed, can never be detected.

THE MAGIC HANDKERCHIEF.

You take any handkerchief and put a quarter or a dime into it. You fold it up, laying the four corners over it so that it is entirely hidden by the last one. You ask the audience to *touch and feel* the coin inside. You then unfold it, and the coin has disappeared without any body seeing it removed. · The method is as follows:

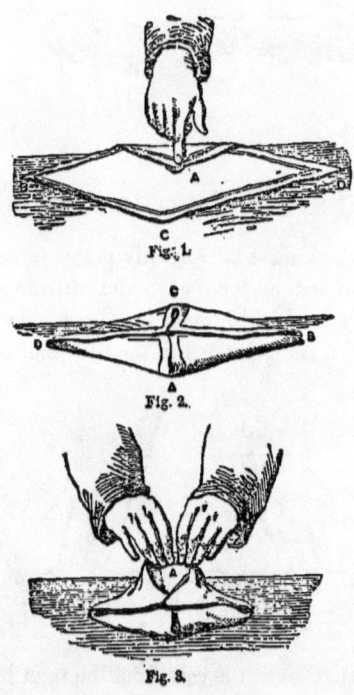

Fig. 1.

Fig. 2.

Fig. 3.

Take a dime and privately put a piece of wax on one side of it; place it in the centre of the handkerchief, *with the waxed side up;* at the same time bring the corner of the handkerchief marked A (as represented in

14

Fig. 1) and completely hide the coin; this must be carefully done, or the company will discover the wax on the coin.

Now press the coin very hard so that by means of the wax it sticks to the handkerchief; then fold the corners, B, C and D (see Fig. 1), and it will resemble Fig. 2.

Then fold the corners, B, C and D (see Fig. 2), leaving A open. Having done this, take hold of the handkerchief with both hands, as represented in Fig. 3 at the opening, A, and sliding along your fingers at the edge of the same, the handkerchief becomes unfolded, the coin adheres to it, coming into your right hand. Detach it, shake the handkerchief out, and the coin will have disappeared. To convince the audience the coin is in the handkerchief, drop it on the table, and it will sound against the wood. This is an easy trick.

THE HAT AND QUARTER TRICK.

Place a hat, tumbler and quarter as represented in the cut; then after making several feints, as if you intended to strike the hat upon the rim,

give the hat a sharp quick blow upon the *inside of the crown* and the coin will fall into the tumbler. This is a beautiful trick if skillfully performed.

1

THE MAGICAL KNOT.

A very amusing trick, consisting of simply tying one knot with two ends of a handkerchief, and by apparently pulling the ends, untying them again. Take two ends of the handkerchief one in each hand, the ends dropping from the inside of your hands. You simply tie a simple knot,

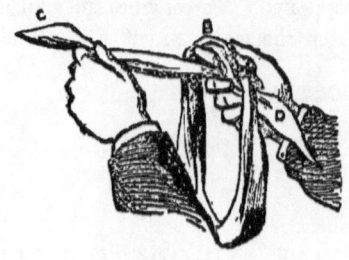

when your hands and your handkerchief will be in the position shown in the cut. Instead of pulling the ends C and D, grasp that part marked B with your thumb and forefinger, dropping the end D, and pulling upon the end C and the bend B, when, instead of really tying, you unloosen the knot.

TO CAUSE A DIME TO APPEAR IN A GLASS.

Having turned up the cuffs of your coat, begin by placing a cent on your elbow and catching it in your hand. That easy feat performed, allege that you can catch even a smaller coin in a more difficult position. Then place a dime half-way between the elbow and the wrist, as in the illustration; suddenly bringing the hand down, the coin drops into your cuff, unseen by

any one, and you express the greatest astonishment at its disappearance. Tell the audience to watch, and they will see it drop through the ceiling. Then take a tumbler, place it at the side of your arm, and elevating the hand for the purpose, the coin falls jingling into the tumbler, causing great marvel as to how it came there.

THE ERRATIC EGG.

Transfer the egg from one wine-glass to the other, and back again to its original position, without touching the egg or glasses, or allowing any person or any thing to touch them. To perform this trick all you have to do is to blow smartly on one side of the egg, and it will hop into the next glass. Repeat this and it will hop back again.

THE OBEDIENT DIME.

Lay a dime between two half-dollars, and place upon the larger coins a glass, as in the diagram. Remove this dime without displacing either of the half-dollars or the glass. After having placed the glass and coins as

indicated, simply scratch the table cloth with the nail of the forefinger in the direction you would have the dime to move, and it will answer immediately. The table cloth is necessary; for this reason the trick is best suited to the breakfast or dinner table.

THE MAGIC EGG.

Take a pint of water and disolve in it as much common salt as it will take up. With this brine half fill a tall glass, then fill up the remaining space with plain water, pouring it in very carefully down the side of the glass or into a spoon to break its fall. The pure water will then float upon the brine, and in appearance the two liquids will seem as but one.

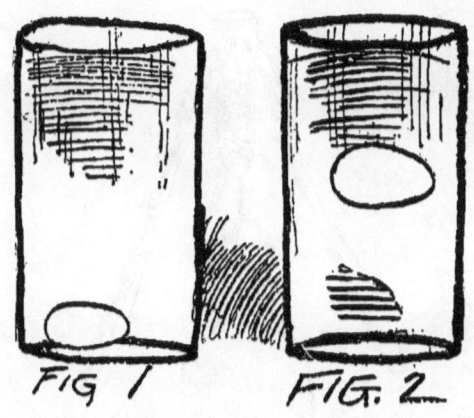

FIG 1   FIG. 2

Now take another glass snd fill it with water. If an egg be put into this, it will instantly sink to the bottom, as in Fig. 1, but if on the contrary, the egg is put into the glass containing the brine, it will sink through the plain water only, and float upon that portion which is saturated with salt, appearing to be suspended in a very remarkable manner, as in Fig. 2.

THE BALANCED COIN.

This engraving represents what seems to be an astounding statement, namely, that a quarter or other piece of money, can be made to spin on the point of a needle. To perform this experiment, procure a bottle, cork it, and in the cork place a needle. Now, take another cork, and cut a slit in it so that the edge of the coin will fit into the slit; next, place two forks in the

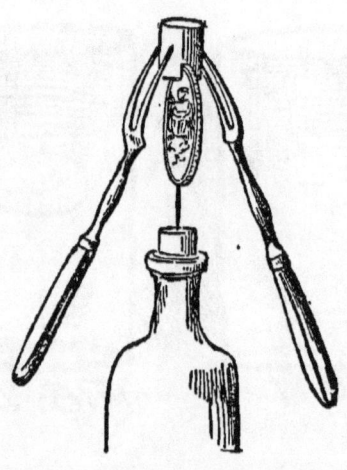

cork, as seen in the engraving, and, placing the edge of the coin on the needle, it will spin round without falling off. The reason is this: that the weight of the forks, projecting as they do much below the coin, being the centre of gravity of the arrangement much below the point of suspension, or the point of the needle, and therefore the coin remains perfectly safe and upright.

THE BIRD WILL GO INTO THE CAGE!

Directions: Place one edge of a visiting card along the line between the bird and the cage, and rest the tip of your nose against the other edge of

the card. Hold the card so that no shadow falls on either side. Watch the bird a moment, and you will see it go into the cage.

THE OLD MAN'S FACE

Is also a very comical amusement and productive of much merriment. The only requisite for producing it is a person's hand, a handkerchief, and a

little Indian-ink. The engraving will show the simplicity of the arrangement, and demonstrates how easy it is to form an old man's face.

STABBING A PENNY.

Doesn't it seem impossible to bore a needle through a penny, particularly if the former is very fine? Yet this is a simple task and is accomplished in the following manner:

The needle is passed through a cork, with the point protruding just a bit, which is then nipped off with a pair of pincers. The penny is then laid upon two little blocks of soft wood, with a small space between, as

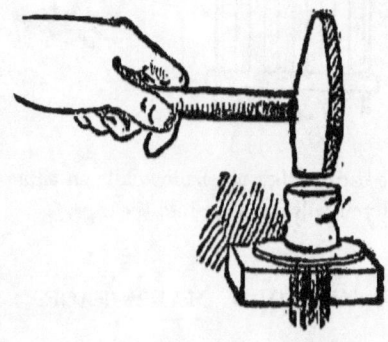

shown in the accompanying illustration. The cork is placed on top of the penny and hammered hard with a small tack hammer. As the cork prevents the needle from springing sideways, the latter cannot fail to pierce the penny, or any other coin of the same thickness, the steel of which the needle is made being harder than the metal of which the coin is composed.

PUZZLES.

THE SQUARE AND CIRCLE PUZZLE.

Get a piece of cardboard, the size and shape of the diagram, and punch in it twelve circles, or holes, in the position shown. The puzzle is to cut the cardboard into four pieces of equal size, each piece to be of the same shape, and to contain three circles without cutting into any of them.

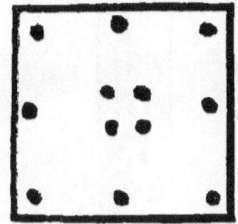

THE MAGIC OCTAGON.

Procure a good stiff piece of cardboard, and draw four each of the three designs represented in the accompanying diagram. If joined together correctly they will form an octagon.

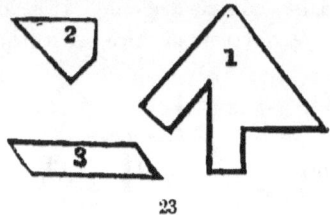

THE BUTTON PUZZLE.

In the centre of a piece of leather make two parallel cuts with a pen-knife, and just below a small hole of the same width; then pass a piece of string under the slit and through the hole, as in the figure, and tie two

buttons much larger than the hole to the ends of the string. The puzzle is to get the string out again without taking off the buttous.

THREE-SQUARE PUZZLE.

Cut seventeen slips of cardboard of equal lengths and place them on a table to form six squares, as in the diagram. It is now required to take away five of the pieces, yet to leave but three perfect squares.

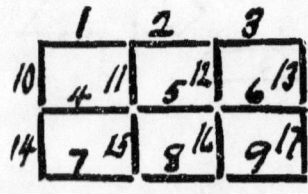

24

THE BOARD AND BALL.

Get the cover of a small cigar-box, or any other thin board, about five inches long, and cut it out in the shape of the engraving. Then arrange the strings and balls as shown in the same.

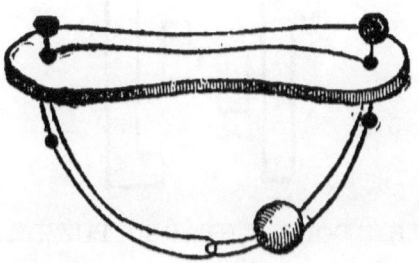

The trick is to get the large ball off the string without removing any of the smaller balls, or untying the string.

CUTTING OUT A CROSS.

How can be cut out of a single piece of paper, and with one cut of the scissors, a perfect cross, and all the other forms as shown in the cuts?

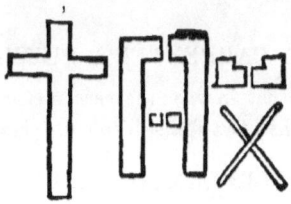

ROMAN CROSS PUZZLE.

With three pieces of cardboard, of the shape and size of No. 1, and one each of Nos. 2 and 3, to form a cross.

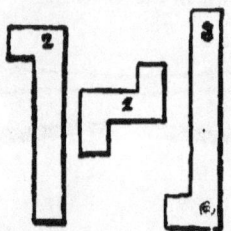

THE DOUBLE-HEADED PUZZLE.

Cut a circular piece of wood, as in the cut No. 1, and four others like No. 2. The puzzle consists in getting them all into the cross-shaped slit until they look like Fig. 3.

THE CARPENTER'S PUZZLE.

A plank was to be cut in two; the carpenter cut it half through on each side, and found he had two feet still to cut. How was it?

THE PERPLEXED CARPENTER.

There is a hole in the barn floor, just two feet in width and twelve in length. How can it be entirely covered with a board three feet wide and eight feet long, by cutting the board only once in two?

WHICH IS THE LONGER?

Just look for a moment at these two horizontal lines, and tell which is the longer. Our friend Snap Judgement will say, "The lower one, of course," but if S. J. will only measure the two he may open his eyes.

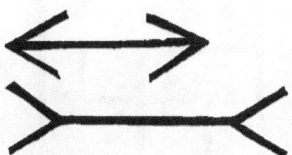

THE STRING AND BALLS PUZZLE.

Get an oblong strip of wood or ivory, and bore three holes in it, as shown in the cut. Then take a piece of twine, passing the two ends through the holes at the extremities, fastening them with a knot, and thread upon it two beads or rings as depicted above. The puzzle is to get both beads on the same side without removing the string from the holes or untying the knots.

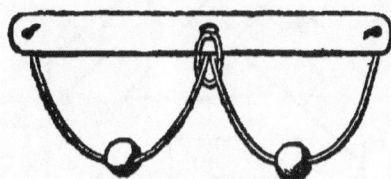

THE ACCOMMODATING SQUARE.

Make eight squares of cardboard, then divide four of them from corner to corner so that you will now have twelve pieces. Form a square with them.

THE THREE RABBITS.

Draw three rabbits, so that each shall appear to have two ears, while, in fact, they have only three ears between them.

ANSWERS TO PUZZLES.

ANSWER TO SQUARE AND CIRCLE PUZZLE.

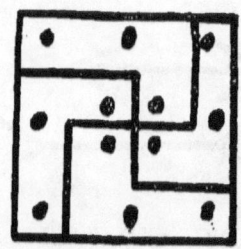

ANSWER TO THE MAGIC OCTAGON.

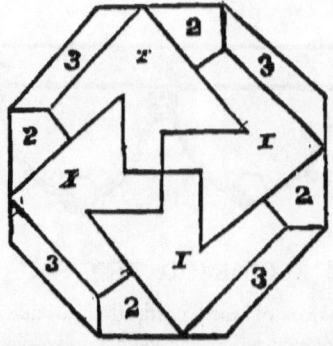

ANSWER TO THE BUTTON PUZZLE.

Draw the narrow slip of the leather through the hole, and the string and buttons may be easily released.

ANSWER TO BOARD AND BALL PUZZLE.

Push the ball close up to the wood and pull the loop of string down through as much as it will come; then pass the end of the loop through the hole in the wood and over the pellet, as here shown. The two loops will then separate and the ball can be easily taken off.

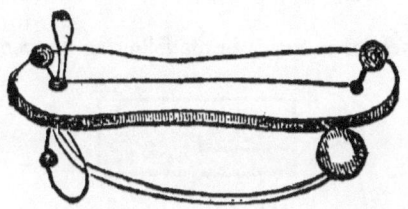

ANSWER TO CUTTING OUT A CROSS PUZZLE.

Take a piece of writing paper about three times as long as it is broad —say six inches long and two inches wide; fold the upper corner down, as shown in Fig. 1; then fold the other upper corner over the first, and it will appear as in Fig. 2; you next fold the paper in half, lengthwise, and

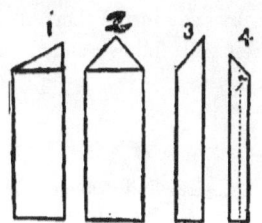

it will appear as in Fig. 3. Then the last fold is made lengthwise also, in the middle of the paper, and it will exhibit the form of Fig. 4, which, when cut through with the scissors, in the direction of the dotted line, will give all the forms mentioned.

ANSWER TO THE THREE-SQUARE PUZZLE.

Take away the pieces numbered 8, 10, 1, 3, 13, and three squares only will remain.

ANSWER TO PERPLEXED CARPENTER.

The plank was cut as shown in the following diagram:

and placed together thus:

ANSWER TO DOUBLE-HEADED PUZZLE.

Arranging them side by side in the short arms of the cross, draw out the centre-piece, and the rest will follow easily. The reversal of the same process will put them back again.

ANSWER TO THE CARPENTER'S PUZZLE.

The plank was sawed as shown in the above cut.

ANSWER TO ROMAN CROSS PUZZLE.

The above diagram will explain to our juvenile friends the puzzling paradox of the Roman Cross.

ANSWER TO THE STRING AND BALLS PUZZLE.

Draw the loop through the central hole, and bring it through far enough to pass one of the balls through. Having done this, draw the string back and both balls will be found on the same side.

ANSWER TO ACCOMMODATING SQUARE.

ANSWER TO THE THREE RABBITS.